Bethany
the Ballet
Fairy

For my cousin Becky,
who could outwit the goblins every time.

Special thanks to Narinder Dhami

No part of this work may be reproduced, stored in a retrieval system, or transmitted in any form or by any means, electronic, mechanical, photocopying, recording, or otherwise, without written permission of the publisher. For information regarding permission, write to Rainbow Magic Limited c/o HIT Entertainment, 830 South Greenville Avenue, Allen, TX 75002-3320.

ISBN-10: 0-545-10615-X
ISBN-13: 978-0-545-10615-3

12 11 10 9 8 7 6 5 4 3 2   9 10 11 12 13/0

Printed in the U.S.A.

First Scholastic Printing, May 2009

Bethany
the Ballet
Fairy

by Daisy Meadows

SCHOLASTIC INC.

New York   Toronto   London   Auckland   Sydney
Mexico City   New Delhi   Hong Kong   Buenos Aires

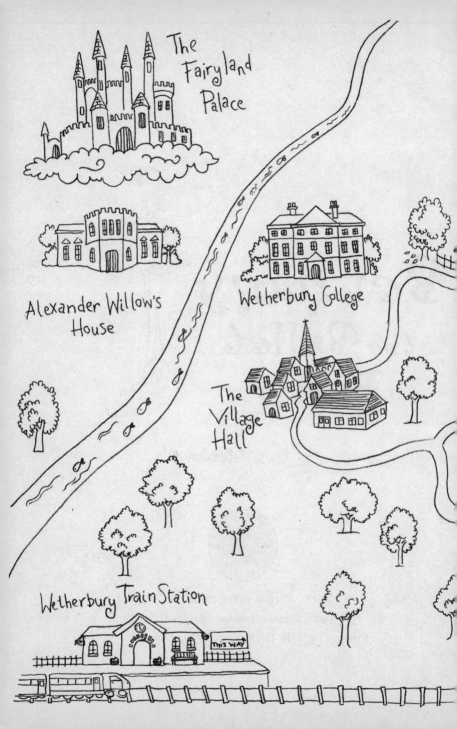

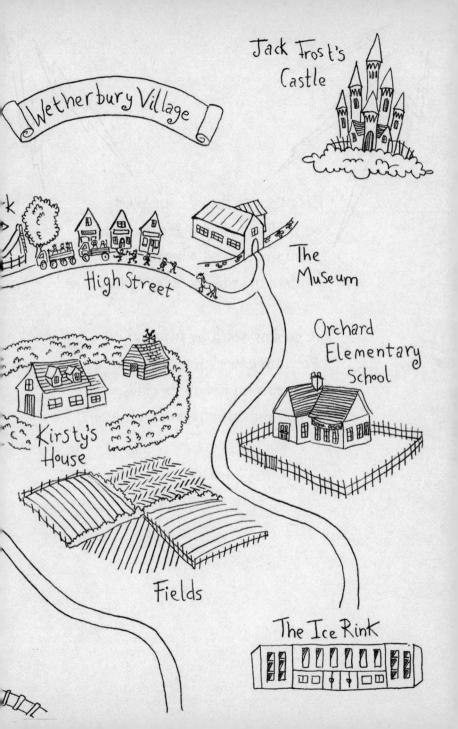

Hold tight to the ribbons, please.
You goblins may now feel a breeze.
I'm summoning a hurricane
To take the ribbons away again.

But, goblins, you'll be swept up too,
For I have work for you to do.
Guard each ribbon carefully,
By using your new power to freeze.

Contents

Fairies in a Whirl

"I'm *really* looking forward to this!" exclaimed Rachel Walker to her best friend, Kirsty Tate. "I *love* ballet."

"Me, too," Kirsty agreed. She raised her voice above the noise of the train as it rattled over a bumpy stretch of track. "I've never seen *Swan Lake* before."

"I've heard that this is an amazing

1

production," Kirsty's mom said. "The
scenery is supposed to be gorgeous."

"Well, let's hope it
keeps Dad awake!"
Kirsty laughed,
glancing at her
dad. He was fast
asleep in the corner
seat. "I'm so glad
you could come,
Rachel. We're lucky that your school
started its vacation the day before ours.
Otherwise, you wouldn't have gotten
here in time."

Rachel nodded. Because their families
lived so far apart, she was staying with
Kirsty for the whole week of school
break.

"We'll be in the city soon," said

Mrs. Tate, as the train pulled into a station. "This is the last stop before we get there."

Kirsty stared out the window as the train slowed down. Suddenly, her eyes were drawn to an icy blue flash that streaked past the window. Curious, Kirsty leaned forward to take a closer look.

To her amazement, she saw seven little fairies tumbling through the air! They were caught in the middle of a tiny, icy whirlwind. As Kirsty watched, the fairies all landed in one of the flower baskets that was hanging from the station roof.

Kirsty and Rachel shared an amazing secret. They were best friends with the fairies! They had often helped the fairies defeat mean Jack Frost and his goblins, who were always causing trouble. Now it looked like their fairy friends might need the girls' help again!

Almost bursting with excitement, Kirsty glanced at Rachel. But she could tell that her friend hadn't spotted the fairies.

"Mom, I'm hungry," Kirsty said quickly. "Do you think Rachel and I could go and get a snack from the dining car?"

Mrs. Tate nodded. "But don't eat too much," she warned. "Remember, we're going out for dinner after the show."

Kirsty nodded as she and Rachel got up from their seats.

"Rachel, I just saw *seven* fairies on the station platform!" Kirsty whispered, as soon as they'd left the train car.

Rachel looked thrilled. "Seven fairies!" she exclaimed. "All at once? Where?"

"Right here!" Kirsty said, pulling down the window right next to the basket where the fairies landed. "Hello!" she called softly, hoping the fairies would hear her.

The fairies were sitting among the pansies and dusting themselves off. At the sound of Kirsty's voice, one of them looked up and saw the girls. She let out a tiny gasp, and a moment later all seven fairies were zooming toward Kirsty and Rachel. They flew inside the train, and Kirsty quickly shut the window.

"You're Rachel and Kirsty!" one of the fairies declared happily. "I've seen you with the king and queen in Fairyland."

The girls smiled at the tiny fairy, who
was dressed in a sparkling
white tutu and pink
ballet shoes.
"Are we ever
happy to see
you," the fairy
went on.
"We're the
Dance Fairies.
I'm Bethany
the Ballet
Fairy, and this is
Jade the Disco
Fairy, Rebecca the
Rock 'n' Roll Fairy, Tasha
the Tap Dance Fairy, Jessica the Jazz
Fairy, Serena the Salsa Fairy, and Isabelle
the Ice Dance Fairy."

Rachel and Kirsty smiled at the fairies. The girls couldn't help but be dazzled by their beautiful outfits. The fairies managed to smile back, but the girls could see that their eyes were sad and their glittery wings drooped.

"Is something wrong?" Rachel asked.

Bethany nodded. "It's Jack Frost!" she announced miserably. "He just cast a spell that sent us all out of Fairyland. That's why we're here, in the human world. But the worst part is that he's stolen our magic dance ribbons!"

Jack Frost Spells Trouble

"Oh no!" Rachel exclaimed. "Jack Frost's up to his old tricks again!"

"What exactly do the ribbons do?" asked Kirsty.

"They make sure that all dancing goes well and is fun, both in Fairyland and in the human world," Bethany explained. "But the ribbons will only work properly if they are each attached to the right fairy's wand. If we don't get our ribbons back, nobody will be able to dance well ever again!"

Rachel and Kirsty stared at each other in shock.

"That's terrible!" Kirsty said.

"Is there anything we can do to help?" Rachel asked.

Bethany smiled gratefully at them.

"Thank you, girls!" she cried. "Even though Jack Frost's spell sent us into the human world, a little bit of fairy magic must have protected us. After all, it brought us here to you! Will you come to Fairyland with us, so that we can tell the king and queen what happened?"

"We'd love to, but what about my mom and dad?" asked Kirsty. "They'll wonder where we are."

"Fairy magic will make sure that, when you return to the human world, no time has passed," Bethany reassured them.

Rachel and Kirsty grinned while Bethany showered the girls with white-and-pink glittering fairy dust. As the magical sparkles floated down around them, the girls shrank to fairy-size. Shimmery wings appeared on their backs.

The next moment, the girls were whisked through the air in a cloud of fairy dust. In no time at all, they were hovering above the golden Fairyland palace.

The king and queen were strolling in the palace gardens. They looked extremely surprised to see the seven Dance Fairies, plus Rachel and Kirsty, fluttering toward them.

"Good afternoon, Dance Fairies!"

King Oberon called. "And welcome, Kirsty and Rachel."

"How are you, girls?" asked Queen Titania, smiling kindly at Kirsty and Rachel. "Do you need our help?"

"No, Your Majesty," Rachel replied, shaking her head.

"It's us, Your Majesties," Bethany declared. "The Dance Fairies need Rachel and Kirsty's help. Jack Frost has stolen our magic dance ribbons!"

The king and queen both frowned.

"He sent us all somersaulting into the human world, too," Bethany went on. "But, luckily, fairy magic led us to Kirsty and Rachel. We all came back to Fairyland to tell you about it."

"Let's see exactly what happened," said Queen Titania, leading the way to the golden pool in the palace gardens. The queen waved her wand over the pool and nodded at Bethany.

The Ballet Fairy immediately touched her wand gently to the water. Ripples began to spread across its surface.

"As Your Majesties already know, Jack Frost was annoyed because whenever he throws a party, none of his goblins can dance properly!" Bethany explained. "So today, Jack Frost asked the all the Dance Fairies to teach the goblins how to dance."

"We thought that maybe Jack Frost had changed his ways and wanted to be friends with us," Jade the Disco Fairy added. "But we were wrong!"

Everyone watched as a picture appeared in the pool. Rachel and Kirsty saw the seven Dance Fairies knocking on the door of Jack Frost's ice castle.

"Are those the magic ribbons?" asked Kirsty, pointing at the fairies' wands in the picture. Each fairy had a ribbon trailing from the tip of her wand. Bethany nodded as the picture changed to show Jack Frost opening the door. His cold, sulky face broke into a smile when he saw the Dance Fairies waiting outside.

"Come in!" he cried. "We're all ready for you!"

Rachel and Kirsty watched as Jack Frost led the Dance Fairies into the throne room. His goblin servants were lined up, dressed in their finest clothes. They wore oversize hats with large feathers, embroidered vests, and velvet

pants. Rachel and Kirsty smiled. They'd
never seen the goblins looking like this
before!

Jack Frost sat on his magnificent ice
throne and watched as the Dance Fairies
began the lesson.

The goblins were *terrible* dancers!

They stumbled across the throne room,
tripping over their own feet, as well as
one another's. Then they started arguing.
Their yelling drowned out the beautiful
music that the Dance Fairies had
conjured up.

But as Rachel and Kirsty watched, the
Dance Fairies quickly began to work
their magic. Gradually, the goblins

stopped bumping into each other and arguing. They began gliding around the room in time to the music, instead.

Kirsty nudged Rachel. "Look, even Jack Frost is enjoying himself!" she pointed out.

Jack Frost was sitting on his throne, merrily tapping his foot along to the music. But suddenly, he jumped up from his seat with a spiteful smile on his face. "NOW!" he bellowed.

Immediately, the goblins dashed forward and grabbed all seven ribbons from the Dance Fairies' wands. Whooping with glee, they began waving the ribbons triumphantly in the air.

The fairies were taken completely by surprise, but they quickly raised their wands to cast a spell.

Unfortunately, they were too late! Jack Frost was already pointing his wand at the fairies, shouting a spell of his own. "Come, freezing wind and ice and snow. To the human world, Dance Fairies, GO!"

Instantly, an icy wind whistled through the throne room. Rachel and Kirsty watched in horror as the Dance Fairies were swept up in the freezing whirlwind and carried out of the window.

"So *that's* how we ended up in the human world." Bethany sighed, as the images in the pool faded. "And that's how Jack Frost got our ribbons!"

Ribbons Whisked Away

"We *must* get the ribbons back," King Oberon declared.

"We'll all go to Jack Frost's ice castle immediately!" Queen Titania decided, waving her wand.

Kirsty and Rachel heard a bell tinkling in the distance. A few moments later the sound of hooves echoed in the air, and a

carriage made of shining crystal pulled
up outside the palace gates. The carriage
was drawn by six unicorns with gleaming
white coats and crystal horns. They came
to a halt, tossing their snowy manes and
neighing softly.

"Look, it's Bertram!" Rachel pointed
out as the king and queen led them over
to the carriage.

Bertram, the frog footman, was sitting at the front of the carriage. He gave the girls a friendly wave.

Kirsty and Rachel climbed in and sat down next to the king and queen on pink velvet cushions. The Dance Fairies perched on the unicorns' backs as the carriage set off through Fairyland.

It wasn't long before they'd left the beautiful green meadows behind. Rachel and Kirsty shivered as the temperature began to fall.

"There's Jack Frost's ice castle," Rachel said. The girls had visited the castle before, but it still looked very scary. It stood on a tall hill under a gloomy sky, and it was made of huge sheets of ice. Its towers were topped with icy blue turrets.

"And there's Jack Frost!" Kirsty added, as a head poked out of one of the windows.

Jack Frost scowled when he saw the carriage approaching. He quickly ducked back inside the castle again.

"Somehow, I don't think he wants to return the magic ribbons!" Rachel remarked.

The carriage pulled up beside the castle, and Bertram hopped down to help everyone out. But as they made their way toward the heavy castle door, it was suddenly flung open. Jack Frost stomped out.

"You're too late!" he snapped. "The ribbons are gone, and there's nothing you can do about it!"

A great shriek above their heads made

Rachel, Kirsty, and all the fairies glance up. They saw a goblin fly out of one of

the castle windows. He was carried through the sky by a giant whirlwind, and he clutched a pink ribbon in one hand.

"That's my magic ribbon!" Bethany cried. She tried to fly toward the shrieking goblin, but the icy wind pushed her back. In fact, the wind was so strong that Rachel, Kirsty, and the others could hardly keep their feet on the ground.

"There are more of them!" Rachel shouted, pointing upward.

Six more goblins were tumbling through the air. Each of them held on to a different ribbon.

"I command you to return the magic ribbons, Jack Frost!" King Oberon cried. Battling against the wind, the king lifted his wand and murmured some magic words. The wind immediately died down, but the goblins had already vanished.

Rachel and Kirsty glanced at each other
in dismay.

"You're coming
with us, Jack Frost!"
King Oberon said
sternly. "And you'll
stay under guard at
our palace until all the
ribbons are returned to
the Dance Fairies."

"Oh, but you'll *never* get the ribbons
back!" Jack Frost cackled. "I've told my
goblins to hide in the human world, and
that's where they will stay! Besides . . ."
he added, pausing and looking even
sneakier than usual. "Even if the fairies
do find my goblins, they'll learn that this
time there's more to them than meets the
eye!" He laughed even louder.

King Oberon sighed and waved his wand again. A swirl of fairy dust lifted Jack Frost off his feet and swept him into the royal carriage.

The doors slammed shut and Jack Frost's smile vanished.

"Girls, the goblins are hiding in the human world with the dance ribbons!" said Queen Titania, turning to Rachel and Kirsty. "Will you help the Dance Fairies get them back?"

Rachel and Kirsty
nodded solemnly.

"Each ribbon is
drawn to its own type
of dance," Bethany
explained. "Each
ribbon's magic will pull
the goblin toward places
where that style of dance is taking
place."

"Oh!" Rachel exclaimed. "We're
going to the ballet tonight. Maybe the
goblin with the ballet ribbon will be
there!"

Bethany looked very excited. "I'll come
with you, just in case!" she said.

Queen Titania was already lifting her
wand to shower them with magic.
"Good luck!" she called.

Looking more hopeful, the other Dance Fairies waved good-bye, as Queen Titania's magic whisked Bethany, Rachel, and Kirsty away. A moment later they were back on the train.

"We'd better go and buy a snack, or Mom will wonder why we're empty-handed!" Kirsty said, as Bethany hid in Rachel's pocket.

"We're almost there, girls," Mrs. Tate said when Kirsty and Rachel returned from the dining car. Mr. Tate had woken up, and they were gathering their things.

Outside the station, they all took a cab to the ballet. As they went into the theater and found their seats, Rachel and Kirsty were amazed to see how beautiful it was. There were tiers of gold balconies, a domed roof painted with ballet scenes, and golden chairs with plush red cushions.

"Are you OK, Bethany?" Rachel whispered as the lights began to dim. Immediately the fairy peeked out of Rachel's pocket and smiled.

The curtain rose, and Kirsty and
Rachel gasped as they gazed at the
wintry scene before them. A
huge frozen lake
surrounded by leafless
trees covered most
of the stage, and
a full moon
hung in
the sky.
Everything
was covered
with frost that
sparkled under
the bright stage
lights. Dancers in
feathery white tutus
were posed here
and there.

"It's beautiful!" Rachel gasped with delight, and Kirsty nodded in agreement.

They waited breathlessly for the ballet to begin, but none of the dancers moved a muscle. Rachel and Kirsty glanced at each other as the audience began mumbling in confusion.

"Why aren't the ballerinas dancing?" whispered Mrs. Tate.

"It's all very strange!" Mr. Tate added.

"Something's not right," Bethany whispered to Rachel and Kirsty. "And I'm sure it has to do with Jack Frost's goblins!"

Frozen!

The dancers still didn't move. The curtain fell, and the whispering of the audience grew louder.

"We have to try to save the ballet!" Bethany said urgently.

Rachel nodded. "We need to find that goblin!" she said.

"Dad, can we go get a program?" Kirsty asked quickly.

Mr. Tate nodded. "Don't be long, though," he said. "I'm sure the curtain will rise again soon."

"We should start looking backstage," Bethany told the girls as they hurried out into the lobby.

"But we need to make sure that no one sees us," Kirsty pointed out anxiously.

They ran to the back of the theater. Cautiously, Rachel pushed open the stage door. A doorman sat in a little booth just inside the entrance. "He's not moving," Kirsty whispered.

"And look!" Rachel added, as they went further backstage. "Neither is anyone else!"

All around them were stagehands who had been moving scenery and dancers who had been warming up. But every single person was now completely frozen in place.

"They're as cold as ice!" Kirsty said, touching one of the dancer's arms. "Maybe Jack Frost has given his goblins a wand of ice magic."

"Listen!" said Bethany suddenly. "I can hear someone giggling!"

"It's coming from the other side of the stage," Rachel said.

The friends hurried across the curtained stage, weaving their way in and out of the motionless dancers. As they neared the other side, they saw a very strange sight.

A goblin wearing pink tights was struggling to get into a fluffy white tutu. He had jammed a pair of dainty white ballet shoes onto his feet, and he had tied a pink bow around his head.

"Oh!" Bethany gasped. "That's my ribbon! It's larger now that it's in the human world, but I'd know it anywhere!"

Rachel and Kirsty put their hands over their mouths to muffle their giggles.

"I thought the goblins were supposed to be hiding," Kirsty whispered. "This one isn't doing a very good job!"

"The magic of the ribbons is so strong that anyone who has one can't help but dance!" Bethany explained, fluttering out of Rachel's pocket. "Come on, let's get my ribbon back!"

The goblin was so busy trying to squeeze into the tutu, he didn't notice Bethany and the girls until they were

right in front of him. Kirsty was glad that
he didn't seem to have a magic wand,
either.

"Give my magic ribbon back, please!"
Bethany said firmly.

The goblin scowled at her. "Go away,
pesky fairy!" he muttered. "I'm not
giving the ribbon back! I like being good
at dancing. And, even better, I'm ruining
the ballet for everyone else! Jack Frost is
going to be *very* happy with me."

"That's mean,"
Kirsty said.

The goblin looked
thoughtful.
Suddenly, he smiled
sweetly at Kirsty.
"Well, OK," he
said. "You can take

the ribbon, but you'll have to untie it for me. I tied it too tightly."

Rachel frowned, feeling suspicious. Why was the goblin being so nice all of a sudden?

"Kirsty, don't —" Rachel began. But she was too late. Kirsty had already stepped forward to undo the ribbon. As she did, the goblin touched her wrist and said, "Freeze!"

Instantly, poor Kirsty was frozen stiff.

Mooning Around

The goblin roared with laughter.

"Oh no!" Rachel gasped, staring in horror at her frozen friend.

"Jack Frost must have given the goblins freezing powers," Bethany guessed. "So that's what he meant when he said there was more to the goblins than meets the eye!"

The goblin stepped forward and reached a big green hand toward Rachel. "Oh, no you don't!" Bethany cried, waving her wand over Rachel and transforming her instantly into a tiny fairy. Rachel zoomed away from the goblin and joined Bethany, out of his reach.

The goblin chuckled. "You can't touch me, or I'll freeze you, too!" Still laughing, he ran onto the stage.

Rachel and Bethany flew after him. "What are we going to do about Kirsty?" Rachel asked anxiously.

"Don't worry, Rachel," Bethany said, as they perched in one of the cardboard trees that was part of the scenery. "The spell will wear off soon, and Kirsty will be fine."

On the stage below them, the goblin had begun to dance. Rachel's eyes widened as he performed perfect jetés, pirouettes, and arabesques.

"He's a wonderful dancer!" she said.

"It's only because he has my magic ribbon," Bethany scoffed. "We have to get it back!"

Rachel watched the goblin move around the stage, and in and out of the wings. He was touching all the ballerinas and stagehands as he went past them, and Rachel guessed he was making sure they all remained frozen.

Suddenly Rachel noticed the large, pale moon made out of tissue paper,

hanging from the top of the stage. It was suspended in the air from a rope. As she looked at it, an idea popped into her head.

"Bethany," she whispered, "if the goblin was underneath the paper moon, we could drop it down to startle him, and grab the ribbon!"

"Great idea, Rachel!" Bethany agreed eagerly. "The moon is very light, so it won't hurt him. But how will we get the goblin to stand underneath it?"

Rachel frowned. Before she could suggest anything, she saw Kirsty hurry onto the stage. Kirsty was keeping a close eye on the dancing goblin, but she was also looking around for Rachel and Bethany. "The freezing spell must have worn off, and Kirsty's looking for us!" Rachel whispered to Bethany. "Maybe she can help us get the goblin underneath the moon."

Bethany nodded. "We'll have to be

careful, though," she whispered back. "We don't want the goblin to guess what we're up to!"

The little fairy waved her wand. A few magic sparkles drifted downward, making Kirsty look up and see her friends in the tree.

Rachel immediately pointed at the moon and then at the goblin, trying to explain to Kirsty that they needed him to stand underneath the moon.

Rachel could see her friend frowning in concentration as she watched. Did she understand what Rachel wanted her to do?

Back on Track

For a moment, Kirsty looked confused. Then she nodded and turned away. "I want that ribbon," she called to the goblin. "And don't even *think* about trying to freeze me again!"

The goblin scowled at her. "I can freeze you any time I want!" he snapped back.

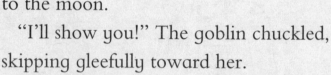

"I don't think so!"
Kirsty said in a
teasing tone.

Rachel and
Bethany watched
hopefully as Kirsty
steadily moved closer
to the moon.

"I'll show you!" The goblin chuckled,
skipping gleefully toward her.

Just a little closer! Rachel thought,
holding her breath. Kirsty took a step

back and the goblin followed,
his hand stretched out to
freeze her. Now he was
right underneath the
paper moon.
With a flick of her
wrist, Bethany sent a burst of fairy

58

sparkles toward the rope that held up
the moon.

The rope untied itself and the moon
dropped down, knocking the goblin to
the floor.

"*Agghh*!" the goblin yelled in surprise.

Quick as a flash, Kirsty whipped the
magic ribbon off the goblin's head. He

sat up, looking furious but not hurt.
Kirsty tried to jump aside as the goblin
grabbed at her wrist, but she wasn't
quick enough. Rachel's heart skipped a
beat as the goblin shouted, "Freeze!"
once again.

But this time, nothing happened!
Kirsty looked
relieved and waved
up at her friends.
"I'm fine!" she called.
Bethany and Rachel flew
down to join her.
"It looks like Jack Frost
only gave you the freezing
power for while you have the ribbon,"
Bethany told the goblin with a grin.

Looking extremely grouchy, the goblin
stuck his tongue out at her. "Well, we

still have the other
magic ribbons!" he
snapped. "And I'll
make sure we hang
onto them!" Scowling,
he jumped up and
ran off.

"Thank you so much, girls!" Bethany
said joyfully. She sent a stream of magic
fairy dust toward the
ribbon in Kirsty's
hand. It floated
over to the little fairy,
shrinking down to
its usual Fairyland
size. As the girls
watched, the ribbon
reattached itself to
Bethany's wand in a cloud of pink

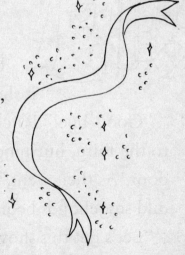

sparkles, shining an even deeper pink
color as it did.

"Now hurry back to your seats while I

fix everything here on
stage," Bethany told
Rachel and
Kirsty. "Everyone
will be unfreezing
soon, and the
performance will
begin. Now that I
have my ribbon back,
it should all go perfectly!"

"Good-bye!" Rachel and Kirsty called
to the fairy, hurrying toward the stage
door. As they went, they saw the dancers
and stagehands beginning to unfreeze.

"Let's get this show on the road!" one
of the stagehands declared.

Rachel and Kirsty grinned at each other. Then they quickly bought a program and dashed back to their seats.

"Just in time, girls!" Mr. Tate whispered as they sat down. "The ballet's starting."

Rachel and Kirsty gazed eagerly at the beautiful scene on the stage once again. The paper moon was back in its proper place, and Bethany was seated on top of it! The little fairy

waved at them before vanishing in a puff
of silvery-white sparkles.

"This is going to be great!" Rachel
sighed happily as the dancers began to
pirouette across the frozen lake on stage.

"But we can't forget that we have six more magic ribbons to find."

"Yes, and we'll have to be careful now that the goblins have new freezing powers," Kirsty whispered. "Still, I can't wait for our next fairy adventure!"

THE DANCE FAIRIES

Bethany the Ballet Fairy has
her magic ribbon back. Now Rachel
and Kirsty must help

Jade

the Disco Fairy!

Join their next adventure in this
special sneak peek!

Girls Go Dancing

"Strike!" cheered Kirsty Tate, as Rachel Walker's ball sent all ten pins flying at the end of the bowling lane.

"Hooray!" Rachel cried in delight.

"That's your third strike today!" Kirsty's dad said, smiling. "Good job, Rachel."

"And it looks like you won the game,

too!" Mrs. Tate added, gazing up at the electronic scoreboard in front of her.

"Yay!" Rachel said. "I'm having the best vacation ever — and it's only just begun!"

"Well, girls," Mr. Tate said as the scoreboard flashed 'GAME OVER.' "It's time to take off your bowling shoes and put on your dancing shoes. You have the school disco tonight, remember?"

"I can't wait," Kirsty said eagerly. "Rachel and I love dancing, don't we?"

Rachel nodded, knowing that Kirsty was thinking about the Dance Fairies!

Once they were back at the Tates' house, the girls got changed in Kirsty's bedroom. Rachel was wearing a pretty purple party dress, and Kirsty picked out

a pink sparkly top and a pair of black pants.

Kirsty picked up a barrette and began fastening it in her hair. Then she stopped and looked at Rachel with a worried expression. "I just thought of something," she said. "What if the school disco is all messed up because the disco ribbon is still missing?"

Rachel bit her lip. "I hope not," she said. "It would be awful if the school dance was ruined. We'll have to look for the goblin and hope that we can get the magic ribbon back to Jade the Disco Fairy before anything goes wrong."

Kirsty nodded. "I don't like the thought of meeting another goblin who can freeze us." She shivered. "But we've got to try and save the disco!"

THE RAINBOW FAIRIES

Find the magic in every book!

SCHOLASTIC

www.scholastic.com
www.rainbowmagiconline.com

HiT entertainme

RAINBO

RAINBOW magic
SPECIAL EDITION™

More Rainbow Magic Fun!
Three Stories in One!

■SCHOLASTIC
www.scholastic.com
www.rainbowmagiconline.com

HiT entertainment

SPFAIRIES

RAINBOW magic

These activities are magical!

■SCHOLASTIC
www.scholastic.com
www.rainbowmagiconline.com

HiT entertainme

RMAC